WHAT A WONDERFUL WORLD

Illustrations by **ASHLEY BRYAN**

PUPPET SHOW TODAY

SATCHMO

By George David Weiss and Bob Thiele
Inspired by the genius of Louis Armstrong

Sundance Publishing

I see trees of green,

red roses too,

I see them bloom

for me and you,

and I think to myself,

"What a wonderful world!"

I see skies of blue

and clouds of white,

the bright, blessed day,

the dark, sacred night,

and I think to myself,

"What a wonderful world!"

The colors of the rainbow,
so pretty in the sky

are also on the faces
of people going by.

I see friends shaking hands, saying, "How do you do?"

They're really saying,
"I love you."

I hear babies cry,

I watch them grow.

They'll learn much more

than I'll ever know,

and I think to myself,

"What a wonderful world!"

Yes, I think to myself,
"What a wonderful world!"